To Ruby,
who inspired me
to design this book.

To my parents,
who enabled me
to complete it.
– E.S.

First published in 2020
by Jessica Kingsley Publishers
73 Collier Street
London N1 9BE, UK

www.jkp.com

Library of Congress Cataloging in Publication Data
A CIP catalog record for this book is available from the Library of Congress

British Library Cataloguing in Publication Data
A CIP catalogue record for this book is available from the British Library

ISBN 978 1 78592 248 0
eISBN 978 1 78450 533 2

Printed and bound in China

Jessica Kingsley Publishers
London and Philadelphia

Let me tell you a story
about a village not so far away...

...a village filled with lots of different
and colourful creatures.

There were the Sproggles,
who loved anything tall and green.

Wearing clothes made out of leaves
was essential, and so was having
dogs for pets.

Then there were the Flinkerdunks, who were square and usually red with anger.
They wore boots and loved riding their bicycles.

The Mimplets were fond of their triangular shapes and blue suited their cool behaviour. They felt very strongly about having cats rather than dogs.

And the Wapsies were round and yellow, like the sun. They baked cupcakes as though their lives depended on it, and you would never find them without their baking hats.

The villagers were creatures of habit.
They each lived in their own
areas and
never
interacted
much
with
each other.

I suppose the only thing the villagers all
agreed upon, was that they did not like
dealing with creatures that were

different.

And so it happened
that these villagers all busied themselves
in their own particular
Sproggly,
Flinkerdunky,
Mimplety
and Wapsie
kinds of ways...

Nothing much ever happened in the village,
and nothing much ever changed,
and this is exactly what the villagers loved about their village.

Until one sunny, sparkly, summery day, a visitor arrived in the Sproggles' part of town...

"Hey there!" said the visitor. "I have come from afar and I have travelled the world, but travelling has made me tired, and I am looking for a place to live."

The Sproggles panicked and hid in their homes.
Before they slammed their doors shut,
one of them shouted:

"You can't live here, you don't even have a dog!"

A little surprised, the visitor moved on to where the Flinkerdunks lived.

“Well, hello!” the visitor said. “I have come from afar
and I have travelled the world, but travelling has made me tired,
and I am looking for a place to live.”

The Flinkerdunks stopped what they were doing, and all gave the visitor an angry look.

"You can't live here, you are not red!" they shouted, and shooed the visitor away.

The day did not feel so sunny anymore. Flustered and shocked, the visitor went to the Mimplets' area.

"So, erm, hi..." said the visitor hesitantly. "I have come from afar and have travelled the world, but travelling has made me tired, and I am looking for a place to live..."

The Mimplets grinned and said:
"You are not cool enough to live here.
And either way, you don't have a cat!"

Confused and irritated, the visitor went to where the Wapsies were.
"Excuse me," the visitor started, "I have come from afar and-"
"We heard you were coming. No baking hat, no home. Now off you go!"

And so the visitor left feeling sad and lonely, but the villagers sighed with relief.
“They were just too different!” said a Sproggle.
“Absolutely – did you see their clothes?” said a Flinkerdunk.
“I say, not cool at all,” said a Mimplet.
“I bet they don’t even like cupcakes!” said a Wapsie. “Well, good day, neighbours!”

Nothing much
ever happened.
Nothing much
ever changed.

And this is exactly
what the villagers loved about their village.

Until that night,
when a big storm came rolling in,
and washed away

all the colours

of the villagers' homes!

The villagers were distraught. They called an emergency meeting to make a plan to rebuild the village, but no one could agree on what their new village should look like.

“I don’t want our homes to be blue!” cried a Sproggle.
“Or round and yellow!” shouted a Flinkerdunk.
“I don’t want dogs in my village!” grumbled a Mimplet.
“It’s not as if cats are so great!” snarled a Wapsie.

“Maybe I can help?” said a voice.
The visitor spoke: “I have come from afar and I have travelled the world. I have seen a lot of different, beautiful places, built by a lot of different, beautiful creatures. I am sure we can build something together that everyone is happy with!”

The villagers quickly huddled back together.
“They are rather strange, but they do sound quite wise,” said a Sproggle.
“They look pretty odd, but their heart seems so kind,” said a Flinkerdunk.
“We have not been so friendly, do you think we have misjudged them?” said a Mimplet.
“We probably have, and we could really do with some help!” said a Wapsie.

And so it began.
Days were spent building,
evenings were spent sharing
and nights were spent sleeping.

Until one sunny, sparkly, summery day, the work was finally done.

10

“It looks different,” said a Sproggle.
“I like all the colours though. I have secretly always wanted a yellow house,” said a Flinkerdunk.
“Me too. And dogs are actually rather cute,” said a Mimplet.
“I think it is splendid! Who knew mixing colours would be so beautiful?” said a Wapsie.

Then they all looked at the visitor.
"Well, I'd better leave you all to it then..." said the visitor.

"Oh, are you leaving?" said a Sproggle.
"That would be sad," said a Flinkerdunk.
"You have rebuilt our village,
and you have given us homes!"
said a Mimplet.
"You are not a visitor anymore.
What may we call you?" said a Wapsie.

"Call me Bobbie," said Bobbie.

“Wonderful! We are sorry we were so mean to you, Bobbie,” said a Sproggle.
“You are a beautiful creature inside and out,” said a Flinkerdunk.
“It would be silly if you left!” said a Mimplet.
“Indeed! Now who would like some colourful food?” said a Wapsie.

And so it happened that all the Sproggles,
Flinkerdunks, Mimplets, Wapsies and Bobbie
lived happily together, in all their beautiful
shapes, colours and patterns.

RAINBOW VILLAGE NEWS
The Funny Case of the Boure and his Farm: p.5

Guide for Parents

By Kate Hutchinson
Regional Officer at Diversity Role Models

The following section contains questions and discussion ideas for reading *Rainbow Village* with a child, or group of children. These questions and discussion ideas will help to highlight the key themes of the story, which are Acceptance, Celebrating Difference, Working Together, Kindness, and Multicultural Society.

They are intended to be used as you read the story and are placed in the order of the book, with some overall discussion points at the end.

page 6 – What do you notice about the houses and the way they are grouped? Why do you think they are grouped in this way?

pages 7/8/9/10/13 – The people are different shapes and sizes and colours but they also have some things that are the same. What colours do we see on the visitor? Are some of those the same colours as the villagers?

pages 15/16 – How do you think the Sproggles feel when they see the visitor and why?

pages 17/18 – Why do you think the Flinkerdunks are angry? Why do you think they have a "Go Away" sign at the entrance to their area? Is that *kind*?

How do you think the visitor feels when they shoo them away? Is it acceptable to push someone like that?

pages 19/20 – What does the doormat say? Do you think it welcomes everybody? How could we change that to include others?

page 21 – One of the Wapsies doesn't look worried or angry – why do you think that is? What are they doing? Is that a kind thing to do?

page 22 – The visitor leaves sad and lonely. Are the reasons they don't welcome the visitor the same as the differences they have with their neighbours?

page 23 – How do you think the visitor feels to be excluded? How many colours can you see in this picture? Why is difference a good thing?

page 27 – What are they all doing? Why are they fighting? If somebody disagrees with you is it acceptable to fight with them? [Fighting is never acceptable.] What could they be doing to change the situation positively?

page 28 – When the visitor returns how do they describe the places and people they have met around the world? [Beautiful and different.] Why are our differences a good thing?

Can you tell me what an opinion is? What is respect? Why do we need to respect people?

page 31 – Can you see what has changed about the villagers now that they are sharing and helping each other?

Why is working together to achieve our goals better than trying to do it on our own?

pages 32/33 – How does the village look different from at the start of the story?

Why is it important for us to learn about and accept each other's differences?

page 34 – One of the Flinkerdunks says "I like all the colours though. I have secretly always wanted a yellow house." Why do you think they never told anyone before? Do you think they were afraid that their other neighbours might have disliked them if they said that before?

If someone feels different from others and is scared to tell anyone that they are different, how could we make things easier for them to be able to talk to someone?

page 36 – We can see all the experiences the visitor has shared with the villagers when helping them rebuild their homes. They have become friends. But the villagers realise they don't know the visitor's name.

If you don't know someone's name, or are unsure if they are a boy, a girl or something else, what should you do and why?

If we have been mean to someone it is always important to say sorry when we are wrong. Why is that?

What things can you see the villagers doing on this page that they were not doing at the start of the story? What does that tell us?

Overall Questions

Which village would you rather live in – the one from the start of the book or the one at the end? Why?

What did the visitor teach the villagers?

Why are people mean to people who are different? Why should they be kind to people who are different?

Can you think of ways people in our street/school/village are different? How should we treat them, even if they are different to us?

Who are Diversity Role Models?

Diversity Role Models, registered charity no. 1142548, have a vision of a world where everybody embraces diversity and can thrive. They create an LGBT+-inclusive environment where students are empowered to embrace difference and end bullying. They embed inclusion and build empathy through education and role model storytelling.

Diversity Role Models operate in the United Kingdom and deliver workshops to students in primary and secondary schools and colleges. The classroom-based workshops are safe spaces where students can explore difference and consider their role in creating a world where we all feel accepted. To ensure sustained change they supplement student workshops with training staff, governors and parents/carers.

Diversity Role Models
Embracing difference, ending bullying

www.diversityrolemodels.org

by the same author

LUNA'S RED HAT

An Illustrated Storybook to Help Children Cope with Loss and Suicide

Emmi Smid

ISBN 978 1 84905 629 8
eISBN 978 1 78450 111 2

Charmingly illustrated, this storybook follows a girl called Luna, whose mother died a year ago. It is designed to be read with children aged 6+ who have been bereaved by suicide to help them cope with their difficult feelings. The book also includes a guide for parents and professionals by grief expert, Dr Riet Fiddelaers-Jaspers.

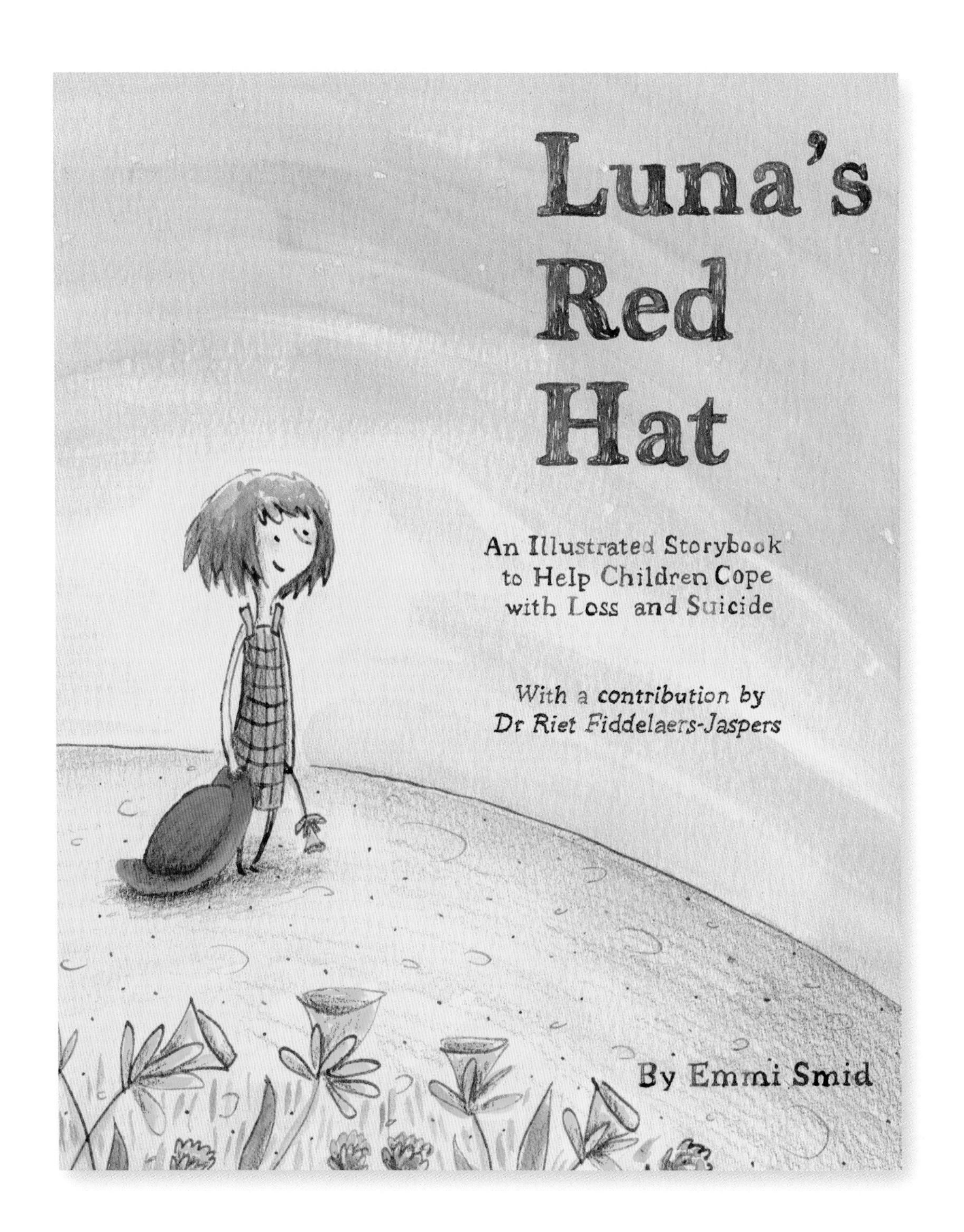

of related interest

You Be You!
The Kid's Guide to Gender, Sexuality, and Family
Jonathan Branfman
Illustrated by Julie Benbassat

ISBN 978 1 78775 010 4
eISBN 978 1 78775 011 1

A House for Everyone
A Story to Help Children Learn about Gender Identity and Gender Expression
Jo Hirst
Illustrated by Naomi Bardoff

ISBN 978 1 78592 448 4
eISBN 978 1 78450 823 4

Phoenix Goes to School
A Story to Support Transgender and Gender Diverse Children
Michelle and Phoenix Finch
Illustrated by Sharon Davey

ISBN 978 1 78592 821 5
eISBN 978 1 78450 924 8